For Paul, who really wants a pet

Henry Holt and Company, LLC
Publishers since 1866
175 Fifth Avenue
New York, New York 10010
mackids.com

Henry Holt® is a registered trademark of Henry Holt and Company, LLC.
Copyright © 2011 by Lauren Castillo
All rights reserved.
Distributed in Canada by H. B. Fenn and Company Ltd.

Library of Congress Cataloging-in-Publication Data
Castillo, Lauren.
Melvin and the boy / Lauren Castillo. — 1st ed.
p.   cm.
Summary: When a boy finds a turtle basking in the sun at the park he thinks he has found
the perfect pet, but the turtle only seems happy at bath time. Includes facts about turtles.
ISBN 978-0-8050-8929-5
[1. Turtles—Fiction. 2. Turtles as pets—Fiction.] I. Title.
PZ7.C2687244Me 2011   [E]—dc22   2010038103

First Edition—2011 / Designed by Véronique Lefèvre Sweet
The art for this book was created using acetone transfer with markers and watercolor.
Printed in March 2011 in China by South China Printing Company Ltd., Dongguan City,
Guangdong Province, on acid-free paper. ∞

10 9 8 7 6 5 4 3 2 1

Melvin and the Boy

Lauren Castillo

Henry Holt and Company ◆ New York

I really want a pet, but I always hear "No."
I ask Mom for a dog like that, but she says, "Too big."

I ask Dad for a monkey like that,
but he says, "Too much work."

I ask for a bird like that, and they both say, "Too noisy!"

Everyone else has a pet.

At the park there is a turtle staring at me.
He has a fancy shell with a yellow spot on top.

He's not too big.
And he won't be too much work.
And he's definitely not too noisy.

"Can I keep him?"
"All right, dear," Mom and Dad agree.
"What will you name him?"
"Melvin," I say. Because Melvin is a good
name for a turtle.

Back home I try to play with Melvin, but he is hiding.

I try to share my snack, but I don't think he likes pretzels.

When I take Melvin outside to meet my friends, he is shy.

He doesn't even want to meet the other pets.

And while I play catch, he tries to sneak away.

When we go out for a walk after dinner, Melvin is very, very slow.

I have to carry him *all* the way home.

When I'm finished with my bath time,
I give Melvin his own bath.
And he finally comes out from his shell!

But he hides again when Dad reads us
a good-night story.
He doesn't want to listen.

In the morning, I tell Mom and Dad that
Melvin isn't having much fun at our house.
    "Maybe he wants
to go back to the
park," I say.

At the park, when I set Melvin free,
he goes right into the pond where two
other turtles are sunbathing.

They look just like Melvin.
"We should let him stay here," I say.

But I make sure to tell Melvin
I can't wait to visit him tomorrow!

Turtle Facts

- There are more than 250 species of turtles.

- Turtles have been on earth for more than 200 million years—they were here before dinosaurs.

- Turtles live on every continent except Antarctica.

- Turtles are reptiles—the only reptile that has a shell.

The top part of the shell that covers the back is called the *carapace*.

The carapace and plastron are joined by a bony structure called the *bridge*.

The outer layer of the shell has hard plates called *scutes*. (They are made of *keratin*, just like our fingernails.)

The bottom part of the shell that covers the belly is called the *plastron*.

- Box turtles (like Melvin) can live for more than 100 years.

- Box turtles live on land, but near streams and ponds. Sometimes they take dips in water to cool off.

- Wild turtles do not thrive well in captivity. In many states it is illegal to remove a turtle from the wild. It is best to observe and enjoy them in their natural habitat.

- Turtles have excellent eyesight and senses of smell. Their hearing and senses of touch are good, too.

- When land turtles are scared, they pull their head, tail, and legs into their shell, which they can clamp shut. Their hinged shell protects them from danger.

- Turtles are measured by the length of their carapaces. The smallest turtle is the bog turtle, which is about four inches long. The largest turtle is the leatherback, which can grow to eight feet long.

Remember to wash your hands before and after handling a turtle to protect each other from illnesses.